In the same series
TOM SAWYER
ALICE IN WONDERLAND

TOM SAWYER

Published in hardback in Great Britain in 2020
by Faros Books Limited, Turret House,
Station Road, Amersham, Buckinghamshire, HP7 0AB

ISBN 978-1-913060-06-0

Text © 2018 Antonis Papatheodoulou
Illustrations © 2018 Iris Samartzi
Translation by Margarita Zachariadou
Edited by Mary Sebag-Montefiore
The right of Antonis Papatheodoulou and Iris Samartzi to be identified
as the author and illustrator of this work has been asserted by them in accordance
with the Copyright, Designs and Patents Act, 1988

A catalogue record for this book is available from the British Library

Printed in Greece
Visit our website at www.farosbooks.co.uk

Mark Twain

Tom Sawyer

or The Largest Playroom in the World

Retold by
ANTONIS
PAPATHEODOULOU

Illustrated by
IRIS
SAMARTZI

FarosBooks

In a very small town on the banks of the Mississippi lives the naughtiest, wildest, unruliest...good boy in America. He lives with his Aunt Polly, his cousin Mary and his half-brother Sid.

-Who ate all the jam out of this jar? asks Aunt Polly furiously.

-Yum...mmmn...not...yum-me, says Tom, his mouth still full and covered with jam. Then he swallows, and, suddenly terrified, he cries:

-Oh, Auntie! Look! What's that behind you? Aunt Polly, very alarmed, twists round. There's nothing at all! But before she's turned back again, Tom has shot out of the front door. The front door, you see, opens to Tom's playroom. It doesn't matter how tiny his house is, because it has the largest, most wonderful playroom in all the world.

The river, the riverbank, the hills, the reeds, the streets and open spaces of his town – all these are Tom's playroom. That's where he finds his fun. He can play hide-and-seek or tag, go fishing or swimming, go climbing or exploring, be a rascal or an imp, join a gang and be a true king of mischief.

When he's with his friends, he can be a treasure-hunter, or a pirate or a riverboat pilot. Today, he's a General. And he's organised a big battle. His army is going to fight Joe Harper's army. Tom and Joe are friends; buddies. And so are their troops. So it's going to be an extremely friendly battle.

You'll take my sword
Now – pull back a little
or you
might get hurt

Attaaaack!
Watch out,
everybody!

Soon the two armies have had enough of winning, and start to dream of... food. That's when the battle is over, and everyone runs home for lunch!
-How did you get your new clothes in such a mess? demands Aunt Polly.
-Fighting, says Tom, and this time there's no escaping Aunt Polly's wrath.

There is no worse punishment for Tom than not being allowed to play with his friends.

Today he's got to paint, all by himself, the whole of the fence around his house.

-Aren't you coming to play with us? asks Ben Rogers.

Tom has an idea. Putting on his most solemn face, he answers,

-Play? Impossible! I have been given the most important job of painting the fence.

It's a very serious undertaking. Not everyone could do it.

-May I try? Just a little bit? I'll give you my apple if you let me have a go.

-Well, all right – only for a moment.

Little by little, all his friends meet up at the fence.

-Let me do some, Tom, and I'll give you my marbles.

-Can I do some too, and I'll give you my kite.

And that's how Tom turns work into play, ending up with all sorts of presents too! He lay back in the shade and had the painting finished as fast as lightning.

Of course Tom didn't stop at chores and punishments. He could turn everything into a game, even learning from books.

-For every ten Bible verses you learn by heart, the minister said, you will receive a little card. And if you work hard, you'll have a Bible as a reward.

Tom had his own method for collecting cards. He went straight to his friends..."My fishing hook for your cards,"... "I'll give you a bag of marbles if you give me two of your cards."

In no time at all, he had a hundred.

-Congratulations, Tom Sawyer, said the minister. You are the most diligent child in the town. Now, since you know so much, tell us the names of the first two disciples of Jesus.

-Eeeer...David and Goliath? said Tom.

What happened next is perhaps better left unsaid.

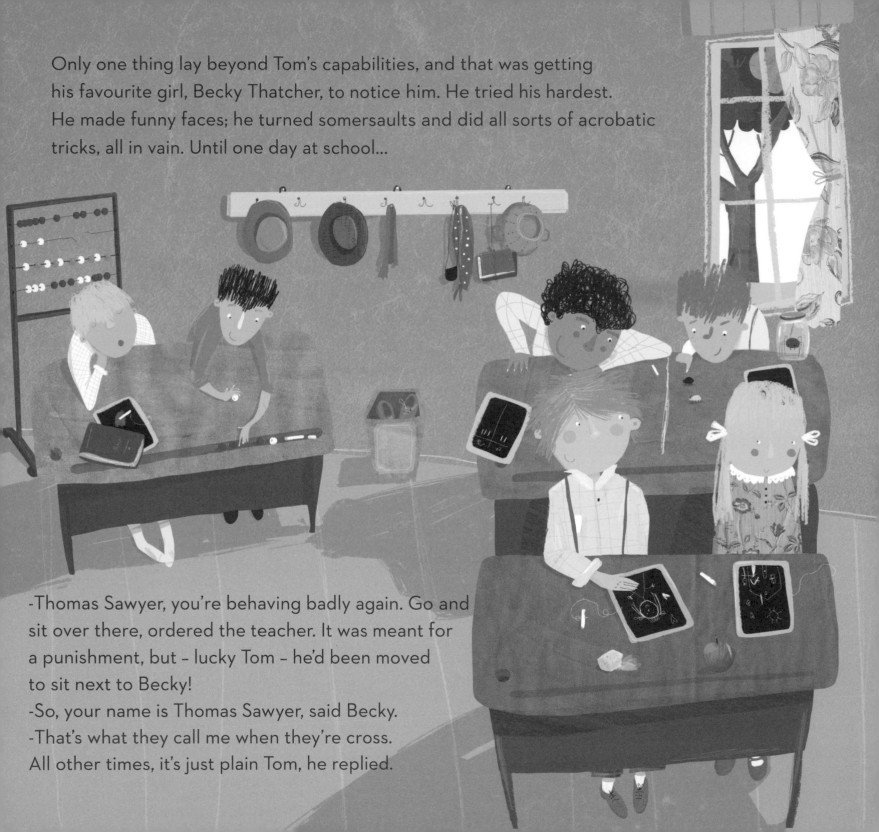

Only one thing lay beyond Tom's capabilities, and that was getting his favourite girl, Becky Thatcher, to notice him. He tried his hardest. He made funny faces; he turned somersaults and did all sorts of acrobatic tricks, all in vain. Until one day at school...

-Thomas Sawyer, you're behaving badly again. Go and sit over there, ordered the teacher. It was meant for a punishment, but – lucky Tom – he'd been moved to sit next to Becky!
-So, your name is Thomas Sawyer, said Becky.
-That's what they call me when they're cross. All other times, it's just plain Tom, he replied.

A few days later, Tom did a truly brave deed that made Becky notice him – and love him. Becky had a passion for books and reading. One day at break time, she opened one of the teacher's books. When she saw him coming back to the classroom, she scrambled to put the book back and accidentally tore one of its pages.

-Who did this? bellowed the angry teacher.

That's when Tom Sawyer stood up and bravely declared:

In the great playroom of outdoors, Tom has many friends, and his best friend is Huck Finn. All the grown-ups think Huck is a rogue and a vagabond. And it's true that Huck is always dressed in shabby, ragged clothes. Instead of going to school, he hangs around the town and roams down to the river, all day.

None of this matters to Tom Sawyer. The two of them are best friends, and Tom sometimes envies Huck's freedom. One afternoon, Tom spied Huck with a dead cat in his arms.

-Where are you taking this poor kitty? asks Tom.

-I found it by the side of the road, and I thought I should give it a respectful burial in the churchyard, replied Huck.
-Why don't you come too?

Tom's playroom, as we know, is full of exciting things. But sometimes they can be dangerous. That night, as Tom and Huck crept to the churchyard, they heard voices. Creeping closer, they saw Injun Joe, the town's most fearsome thug, attacking another man with a knife.
The boys ran away, their hearts beating like drums.

By the next day, the whole town had heard of the crime, and there was a trial. Injun Joe lied in court, and said someone else had done it. Judge Thatcher, Becky's father, called Tom Sawyer to be a witness.

Now, Tom does tell lies, just little ones: "No, Aunt, I didn't eat the jam!" or "I never stole the sugar." But when it comes to an innocent man being convicted, and a guilty man getting away with it, that's a different story. A serious story. So Tom summoned up all his courage and told the truth. He'd seen Injun Joe do the wicked deed. Everyone admired Tom, but Injun Joe managed to escape. He jumped out of the window and disappeared.

For the next few days, Tom was anxious. Becky was away on holiday, and he missed her. And he was scared. Where was Injun Joe? Did Injun Joe want revenge?
There was only one way to conquer his worries.

Play Pirates.

He met his friends by the river. They hauled their supplies
onto their raft, chose their pirate names and off they sailed.
Tom Sawyer, the Black Avenger, commanded "Push off!"
-Full steam ahead! shouted Huck Finn, the Red-handed,
as Joe Harper, the Terror of the Seas, took the oar!

The three friends reached the island. They played, they swam, they fished, they went treasure-hunting, they slept... and then they began all over again.

Suddenly, in the midst of their endless fun, they heard voices from the shore, and saw several small boats coming closer.

-They're probably looking for someone, Tom said, and in a flash the three boys realized the boats were looking for them. They'd been playing pirates so intently that a whole day had gone by, without them noticing. Quickly, they jumped aboard their raft and rowed home.

At last Becky had returned from her holidays. Even better, she had a surprise invitation for Tom. Her parents were planning a picnic party and were asking all their friends, including Tom.

The party was to be held just by the famous MacDougal Cave.
-Let's explore the cave, Tom suggested.
Tom and Becky became real cave explorers.
They discovered underground lakes and waterfalls, and passages leading to echoing halls deep in the caverns of the great cave.

MacDougal Cave

After a while they realized they couldn't hear
the rest of the party any more. They were lost!
-We must stay strong, Tom said.
The two children were very tired. They'd been
wandering for hours. Then Tom heard a voice.

Surely it was their friends who were looking for them!
But listening more closely, Tom froze with fear. It was
the voice of Injun Joe! The MacDougal Cave
was his hideout.

Tom and Becky had to get out of the cave. Tom thought carefully and fast. In his pocket was a spool of fishing line. He gave one end to Becky, and held on to the other end himself.

-Each time I go the wrong way, I'll follow the line back to you. We'll never lose each other. Tom spent the whole night searching. And, at last, at dawn, a ray of light shining through a tiny crack, showed him the way out.

The whole town was overjoyed to see them safe and sound. Judge Thatcher ordered the entrance to the cave to sealed tight shut immediately.

Tom ran straight to the judge the moment he heard the news.

-Sir, Injun Joe is in the cave. You must open it!

Tom would never let any man – even a villain, be trapped in a cave forever.

So they all went back to the cave: the grownups to find Injun Joe, but Tom and Huck to play their favourite game: treasure hunting!

And they found it; piles of money! Of course, Tom and Huck are trained pirates, and if they search for treasure, without a doubt, they'll discover it. Tom and Huck became the richest people in town, so rich that they could have bought all the toys in the world. But why would they want to do that?

Tom and his friends already know the best way to have fun. They could play hide-and-seek or tag, go fishing or swimming, go climbing or exploring, be rascals or imps, join a gang or be true kings of mischief. All they had to do was to open the door to the largest playroom in the world.

Antonis Papatheodoulou was born in Athens. He has published more than 50 books for children, some of which have been translated into eleven languages. They have also been adapted into plays and for puppet theatre and have won many awards, including two Greek State Picture Book Awards and the 2016 International Compostela Prize for Picture Books. Five of his books have been included in the White Ravens list of the International Children's Library of Munich. Discover more about Antonis and his work at www.antonispapatheodoulou.com.

Iris Samartzi is a children's book illustrator and an art teacher. Her work has received many awards, including the 2016 International Compostela Prize for Picture Books, the Greek State Picture Book Award (2012, 2016) and the Greek IBBY Award (2012, 2015, 2016 and 2017). When she is not illustrating books, she runs art workshops for children. She lives and works in Athens, Greece. Read more about Iris and her work at www.irissamartzi.com.

Samuel Langhorne Clemens was the American author known by his pen name Mark Twain. He was born in Missouri in 1835. When he was four years old, Twain's family moved to a town near the banks of Mississippi. The residents and surroundings of the town in which he grew up inspired his works *The Adventures of Tom Sawyer* and *The Adventures of Huckleberry Finn*. Mark Twain travelled all over the world and worked as a coal miner, riverboat pilot, newspaper columnist, printer and publisher. Although he did see his novels become a huge success and earned a great deal of money from them, he took bad investing decisions and came close to bankruptcy. He died in 1910, at the age of seventy four. In 1976 the asteroid 2362 was named Mark Twain in his honour.

MISSISSIPPI